'BEING SEEN
MADE ME
THEIR KING. IT
GAVE ME MY
AUTHORITY, AND
ALL THE PEOPLE
WATCHING
WERE MY
SUBJECTS.'

YUKIO MISHIMA
Born 1925, Tokyo, Japan
Died 1970, Tokyo, Japan

'Star' was first published in Japan in 1961 in a short story
collection of the same name.

MISHIMA IN PENGUIN MODERN CLASSICS:
Confessions of a Mask
Forbidden Colours
Life For Sale (forthcoming)
The Frolic of the Beasts

YUKIO MISHIMA

Star

Translated by Sam Bett

PENGUIN BOOKS

PENGUIN CLASSICS

UK | USA | Canada | Ireland | Australia
India | New Zealand | South Africa

Penguin Books is part of the Penguin Random House group
of companies whose addresses can be found at
global.penguinrandomhouse.com.

First published in the United States
of America by New Directions Books 2019
First published in Great Britain in Penguin Classics 2019
001

Translation copyright © Sam Bett, 2019
All rights reserved

Printed and bound in Great Britain by Clays Ltd, Elcograf S.p.A.

ISBN: 978-0-241-38347-6

www.greenpenguin.co.uk

Penguin Random House is committed to a
sustainable future for our business, our readers
and our planet. This book is made from Forest
Stewardship Council® certified paper.

Star

I glanced into my assistant's little mirror at the crowd gathered in the street.

The fans were relentless. They leaned with all their weight against the ropes, reaching to get just a little closer to me, cheering and screaming to catch my attention.

It was a good crowd, full of pretty girls and boys alike who were skipping work or school to stand here in the bright May sun. Each and every one of them had shown up in the uniform—an ensemble of my own design that I'd singlehandedly popularized. They loved dressing in this uniform for me: the straw hat with a garish ribbon; the short-sleeved shirt with epaulets, stripes taut across the chest, and all three buttons undone to reveal a glinting pendant; slim pants that left no curve or bulge to the imagination, front or back, down to the ankles showing through their sheer black socks. The kids were more or less my age, young and spunky, broke and bored, and flaunting a doomed surplus of energy.

I was their model and their aspiration, the mold that gave them shape. I made a point of remembering this whenever I peeked into my assistant's little mirror. My reflection was boyish and alive, but all the life was in the makeup. Since my face looked a little greasy, I applied some more powder, but I knew that there was nothing shining underneath. My physique was rugged and my build was solid, but the old power was escaping me. Once a mold has finished casting its share of copies, it cools and becomes deformed and useless.

Here I was at twenty-three, an age when nothing is impossible. Yet I knew for certain that the last six months of working days on end with barely any sleep would be the farewell to my youth.

But such foresight came courtesy of the real world. Not my world. Thinking ahead was basically useless to me—no more than a fantasy. I had long since cut ties with that world, like a yakuza stepping out of the game and washing his hands of it once and for all. I had no more use for dreams. Dreaming was for the moviegoers, fingering their pulpy paper tickets. Not for me.

The farmer's daughters in the fan clubs were always asking me, "What's it like to be a star?" It amazed me how these clubs managed to attract so many ugly girls. Sometimes they even had cripples. You'd have a real hard time going out on the street and rounding up a group of girls that ugly. All I'm saying is they could carry on about their own dreams all they wanted, but there was no way I could tell them how it felt to live inside one.

"What shot are we on?"

"Looks like Shot 6."

My assistant showed me a page of the script, marked up with camera blocking in red pencil.

Takahama was the sort of director who blocked

things out precisely. He always planned his scenes the night before, but once we got going he started hoarding details. If something on the sidewalk caught his eye, he forced it into the scene. At the moment he was hung up on getting some scraps of paper to roll and drift down the street artistically, giving me the chance to take a breather.

"Damn, even that trash rolls better than me ..."

I practiced my line for Shot 6 under my breath, trying out different facial expressions in the little mirror. Thanks to these American eye drops I was using to rid the signs of sleep deprivation, my eyes were clear and sharp, in tune with the cheap nihilism of a young yakuza.

"No autographs in the street, please," the assistant director shouted, pushing back against the crowd.

One of the girls yelled "Lighten up!" and everybody laughed. In the corner of the little mirror, the white pages of their autograph books shimmered in the sun.

The mirror darkened: the part of it unoccupied by my reflection was filled in by the sad face of my assistant, Kayo Futoda—my constant companion, day in day out, always ready with my makeup kit and chair. She looked at least forty but was barely even thirty. Her two front teeth were silver, and she wore her hair in a messy bun, with no regard for her appearance. While she let on like she was a moron quite convincingly and pretended not to get things, Kayo was in fact my accomplice, my partner in this artifice. To be honest, she was probably the better actor.

I saw the moon in Kayo's silver teeth. When she laughed in the dark they flashed like tabs of moonlight. Sometimes I had to touch them, to be sure of what they were, and felt better confirming they were fakes.

Then again, I'd never touched the moon. For all I knew, its surface felt the same as Kayo's teeth. If the moon were actually silver, these could be pieces of the real thing. But fakes were what I really wanted.

"Don't make fun of my teeth. I owe everything to them. Who would ever want to kiss me after seeing these?"

She boasted of her flaws as if they were assets, but Kayo would never tell you being ugly made her safe.

Kayo believed in me more than I believed in myself. She was the one who quenched my thirst for love. One night, back home after a long evening of filming, I was sitting on my bed in tears, reliving the reaming the director had given me that day. Kayo came in and soothed me, cried with me, and began to rub my shoulders, then started working all around my body. Before I knew it, we were sleeping together.

From then on, our intimacy required no emotion. We were in on the same joke and basked in the shared pleasure of mocking and backstabbing the world around us. But Kayo still gave me those massages. She made a game of it, like she was sizing me up.

"And here we have Rikio Mizuno's shins! So smooth, so hard."

Sometimes, just to tease me, Kayo called me her "Little White Lily Bud." If anyone else messed with me like that I'd kill the asshole straightaway, but from Kayo it was nothing. She was certain that my "little lily bud" was what made me so insecure in our affair. She wasn't altogether wrong.

When we were done in bed, we would gaze through the gap in the curtains onto the dark street below the house.

Even late at night, it wasn't strange to see a half-crazed fan hiding in the shadow of a telephone pole, peering up at the light of my bedroom window. They knew the whole layout of the house, from where my parents slept, to Kayo's room, down to the kitchen. Because we couldn't let ourselves be seen, not even as a shadow on the shades, we stood the lamp up just inside the window.

All we could do was poke our faces through the tiny gap between the curtains and sip away at the night air, heady with the smell of new leaves. This was my meager daily dose of nature, but like strong sake it didn't take much to make me tipsy.

"That pavement's the border of the world. As long as they can't see us from down there, they can't see us from anywhere. It's funny, really. We're safe inside this big old lie."

Our relationship was actually very abstract. Of course the world was partially to blame, but there was also something inside of me, a tendency that egged it on. And Kayo had it too, in the dim light of the bedroom, drunk off her own ugliness and our charade. Sometimes she gave voice to the absurdity: "And here we have Rikio Mizuno's chest, and here I am, Ms. Futoda, with my cheek nuzzled up against it. Who'd ever believe that?"

We were different people, and there was nothing remotely natural or even plausible in our partnership, but operating contrary to expectations and remaining ever-conscious of the act gave both of us a mainline to euphoria. This made the secrecy of the affair absolutely crucial. My parents looked the other way, but Kayo still took every precaution in maintaining the ruse. Not because she feared a scandal, but for the pure satisfaction of consummate deceit.

The fact that every woman out there wanted me but couldn't have me gave Kayo, in her secretive monopoly, the sick pleasure of being the exception. Her ugliness was everything, and she made it plain. Like a saint, she showed her age without apology, not hiding it from me or anybody else. The lie was all we ever needed.

Kayo never gave a thought to jealousy.

Every day she went through the entertainment magazines and weeklies strewn about my bedroom, cut out every column or interview that I appeared in, and diligently pasted the clippings into a scrapbook. Her favorites were the photographs of me chatting with gorgeous actresses, the gossip columns about me and gorgeous models, and the endless debates over who I was going to marry.

"This one says you're engaged to Midori Masaki. Hah! That's a laugh. Everybody knows her uterus is chronically inflamed."

Most of all she loved the interviews where I was asked about the type of woman I preferred. She found one called "A Dreamboat's Musings on the Ideal Girl" and began to read aloud: "I'm a sucker for a pretty face, but I'm especially drawn to slimmer pixie types. And there's something irresistible about a woman's ankles …"

"Perfect!" she said. "Stick with that. There's no need to be hopelessly romantic. Modern stars need to speak in a way that clearly frames the woman as a sex object."

"Watch out, or they'll switch you to the PR Office."

"How about my ankles, Rikio?"

Kayo shook off one of her slippers, gestured her leg in the air like an Indian dancer, and presented me with her bare foot. The knob of her girthy ankle was tough, rugged, and discolored. If the ankle of a girl is like an almond in a thin, delicate skin, Kayo's was a big brown chestnut. What makes a woman's ankles beautiful is this immodesty, the sudden appearance of something animalistic along the otherwise smooth leg, yet Kayo's ankles were like knots in old wood, the evidence of some oppressive natural law.

But I can't say I felt anything like disgust—that was for the real world, the world I had forsaken.

I lifted Kayo's foot with one hand and met her ankle with my lips. It went limp, lost its stiffness and its dryness, and became a giant yellow rose, or the face, carved from boxwood, of a meditative buddha. It gave off a smoldering light and took on subtle undulations. The presence of cool bone was palpable beneath the skin, and I imagined it was bare bone I was kissing.

At that moment I kissed the essence of my fallacy. This was the very core of my existence, and the ultimate expression of the world that I had chosen, the world where I belonged. It was something no one else had ever tasted.

Kayo squealed and pulled her foot away—she saw straight through my most obscure emotions.

"Playtime's over, little prince," she said. "You'll always be my handsome little prince, even when you're sixty."

"Let's do it, Richie."

The second assistant director walked over to where I sat. "Richie" was the cutesy nickname favored on set and among my fans.

I looked away from the little mirror, handed it to Kayo, and stood up.

We were shooting at the busy center of a suburb, in a neighborhood along one side of an elevated railroad. The embankments leading up to the tracks were covered with grass, but trash was piled at the bottom of the slope, and scraps of litter tangled in the shallow roots. The sunlight inside of a tin can shimmered on a little pool of yesterday's rain.

On this side of the tracks there were cheap bars and saloons. It was the middle of the day; everything was closed, but the windows were full of faces, locals peeking out to catch a free show whenever the camera was pointed away. Outside, the fans pushed and shoved behind the ropes strung up on both sides of the street.

With my striped shirt barely buttoned, I slung my jacket over my shoulder.

The cinemascope camera was perched on a wooden tripod, its lens pointed at the road.

When we were filming, Takahama was always squatting by the camera. He was lanky, skeletal, and had a long, hyperactive nose and a tiny little mouth. His whole face was darkened from incessant exposure to the brutal world of dreams. Habitually dismissing the commotion of his surroundings to give himself the space to think, his gaze was lonely and parched, a gaze most people could never wear in public. It felt so private, like something I was never meant to see. He had the eyes of a child locked naked in a secret room.

"We'll open with you over there," he said, almost talking to himself, and stood from his crouch, clutching the script.

"You kick the empty can into the air. Water goes flying. The camera tilts up. Then you say ... what'd we say?"

"Damn, even that trash rolls better than me."

"Right. At the end of the line, on 'better than me,' we'll dub in the whoosh of the train. Squint like you're annoyed. That'll do it."

We got ready for the test run. Because the camera couldn't catch the water in the can effectively, the assistant director had to crouch down on the ground and painstakingly adjust the way it pointed. There were peaches on the label. With its jagged lid flipped up, the blown-out can looked awfully solemn.

It should come as no surprise, but whenever we're filming on location, whether in a town like this or somewhere way off in the mountains, "nature" is nowhere to be found. After passing through the camera, the scenery is no more than a dense collection of objects. Alluring forests or mesmerizing temples separate into their various constituents, with every scene a garbage dump of information, another miscellaneous, wild heap of things that are cold, or dark, or twinkling, or stagnant, a confusion of unmanageable shapes. Amid all this, some trivial or unlikely object—like a broken bottle in a wall of garbage—declares its splendor.

"Try not to hit this thing with your foot during the test run," the assistant director told me.

"Which direction am I supposed to kick it?"

"That depends …"

"Up!" cried Takahama. "It's gotta be up! Otherwise the water won't go anywhere. Alright! Test!"

Takahama was already on edge. Maybe he'd been cursed by the tumbling scraps of paper.

Every time the train whooshed above us during the test run, I squinted in a way that failed to satisfy.

"It doesn't look like you're annoyed. Looks like you're squinting at a light that's shining in your face. That's not gonna cut it. Try not to let your eyes close. It's not like you've suddenly gone blind or something. Alright? … You're squinting because of the train, but your face has to make sense with the previous line. You're not even thinking about the train. What train?"

I found myself adrift in the lonely expanse that an actor enters upon being criticized, but I remained enveloped in my role as if it were an invisible skin, close and protective. It traced the contours of my mind and body, wafted up like ether, shielding me from reality. I may as well have been behind a castle wall. Even if the director lost his temper and threw a punch at me, his fist would swim through unreal air and never actually hit me. I knew this, I was certain, but the real world has no parallel for such certainty.

After the test run, we were finally ready to shoot. Everything depended on the train, and since I had to do the lead-up with my back turned to the tracks, it was going to be difficult to time. I had measured it by listening to the train as it crossed the overpass and approached the tracks above us.

"What time's the next one?" Takahama asked.

"3:18, on the dot," the assistant director answered. "Or rather, that's when it reaches the station. It should hit the overpass at 3:16 and thirty seconds."

"Alright, start shooting when it hits the overpass."

The assistant director hushed the crowd with his megaphone.

"Quiet down, please, we're about to begin."

Kayo came over with the little mirror. Her shoddy black slacks, snug at the thighs, barely contained her ample hips. I glanced in the mirror and then gave it back to her. She looked over my face as if inspecting fabric for imperfections.

The train appeared, tiny in the distance, riding through the liquid sunlight. The tracks above began to hum.

"Ready!"

The assistant director stood in front of the camera and fanned open a clapperboard with SCENE 16, SHOT 6 written on it in chalk.

The train rumbled across the overpass.

"Action!"

There was the whir of silent film, like vapor hissing from a leak. The clapper slapped and pulled away.

We were back in the surge of imaginary time. No matter how many scenes we'd already filmed, once I was behind the camera with the film unspooling, time flowed like the cool, clear waters of a high ravine, where I could swim my way upstream. My body took on buoyancy, and even walking the same ground as before felt like something more than walking. I became the force of time incarnate, following a steady rhythm, passing through the scripted motions one by one like they were floating weeds that curled around my body and slipped off of me and drifted away. Compared to this variety of time, the hours of ordinary life were no more than a worn and tattered obi unwinding from the waist.

Now I could be seen completely. Being seen made me their king. It gave me my authority, and all the people watching were my subjects.

Eyes, countless as the gravel at a shrine, pressed in all around me. They found their center—my image coalesced. In that moment, dressed as a yakuza, I became a sparkling apparition, like a scepter thrust against the sky.

This apparition is ravaged by the business of the performance. The lines, the gestures, the way I touch the props, the point in the dialog where I adjust my posture ... each delicate move is crammed into a few seconds, with no choice but for me to go from this to that, moving nimbly and naturally as a butterfly inspecting a bed of flowers.

In elementary school, we had to take an IQ test just like this.

"Ready? Pick up this book, head over to that desk, open up the drawer, put the book inside, take the paperweight and the hat off of the desk, hang the hat on that hook, and bring me just the paperweight. Sound good?"

I kicked the can. The toe of my shoe sent it flying, in a clean arc. Water flew like sparks. The camera tilted up. As I watched the angle shift from high to low, I let my body burn with energy, and prepared my expression, the scowl before I click my tongue and deliver "Damn ..."

You can't rush through your lines. Especially when you're on location. If you get worked up and start jabbering away, it's impossible to add them in during the overdub.

"Damn, even that trash rolls better than me ..."

I said the line with a hollow stare and knew I'd nailed it. On cue, the train rushed overhead, crackling like a shower of steel. I had decided that before I squinted, I would look up toward the train out of the corner of my eye, and did just that—squeezing my left eye just a little harder than the right.

"Cut!" yelled Takahama.

The set was silent.

"OK!"

When Takahama said OK but didn't mean it, the word would barely leave his throat. Those within his circle understood that even a mumbled OK could have a multitude of nuances. This time around, however, his OK didn't sound so bad.

The tension dissipated. When I sauntered back over to the folding chair that Kayo pushed toward me, the crowd rejoiced like I had just returned from war.

"That last take was just great. Two shots left. Want some tea?"

Kayo held out a metal thermos. Its polished surface was smeared with the faces of the crowd. She popped it open for me. Steam huffed from the bottle and fogged the metal around its mouth. I felt my confidence about the last take fogging over.

"It was a great take," Kayo repeated unconcernedly. "The way you squinted when the train went by was absolutely perfect. If you can keep it up I'm sure we'll be OK."

"Two more shots …"

And after that another night of filming. At this point it felt like my body was coming apart from lack of sleep.

"Richie! Richie! Sign mine!"

Girls were yelling from the crowd. I smiled at them and gave a little wave.

"He saw me!"

"Over here!"

I was exhausted. The girls could scream like hell for all I cared—their shrill voices splashed over me like rancid oil. If only I could line them up and march them all into the mouth of an incinerator. Except they'd probably crawl out of the ashes gawking at me, so I'd have to pluck their eyes out first.

"Two more shots …"

I lost control and yawned.

"Look! He's yawning!"

Neriko Fukai, who was acting opposite me, had gone home hours earlier, leaving me on my own for the two remaining shots. Lately she was in such high demand that we had to film all of our scenes together in the first half of the day.

The shot right after this one, where Neriko shows up and says—"What, talking to yourself again?"—had been over and done with since morning. It'd only been a few hours, but the little I remembered was already starting to fade.

2

Kayo loved sorting through my fan letters. She worked quickly, but we never made much progress—whenever she found a real sidesplitter, she stopped to read it aloud. These letters were usually from widows, like the woman who described her fantasies of sex with me in pimply detail, or from perverts, like the guy who desperately wanted me to send him my underwear.

When Kayo was tired of the letters, she helped me think up tales of young romance to prepare me for the interviews. To keep things interesting, she insisted that I always tell a different story, with a first love at age seven, another at ten, one for fifteen, one for seventeen. It goes without saying that each account had to be innocent and pure, in keeping with the vision of the PR Office.

My job was to come up with a backstory of violence. I'd been a shy kid. All I did was draw. I never came close to fighting anybody. Instead of gambling with the other kids, I chose the blue sky, and treasured not the gold leaf on their playing cards, but the golden sundown rimming actual young leaves. Looking back, I can say that loving nature was an error. Not seeing my affection for the weakness that it was, I put a stain upon my youth.

This hour before sleep was my only break during the entire day. After bathing, I wrapped myself in a bathrobe and lay on the sofa by the window, where I listened to the late-night jazz programs and occasionally exchanged a few words with Kayo, who sat on the floor with the letters fanned around her.

Sometimes Kayo came over to the sofa and snuggled up beside me.

"Who should I do tonight? Natsuko Suzaku? Remember that ravishing kiss?"

"Let's see it."

Kayo did her impression of the famous actress in the one kiss scene we'd shot together. Coming from Kayo, it was pure caricature. She flared her modest nostrils to mimic Natsuko's grand nose, bared her silver teeth, and let her mouth fall open, as if dreaming. Quivering her lips, she drifted her hand to the back of my head and pulled me in, stopping just a breath away, but not for long. When the time was ripe, she lowered her fake eyelashes, gazed down her nose, and snapped her lips to mine with the pull of a magnet.

"The End."

We both laughed.

"Want me to do Misao Yawata?"

"Sure."

Misao was a popular young actress I'd starred opposite recently.

With a pinch of her bun, Kayo undid her impossibly long hair. Kneeling beside the sofa, she buried her face in her hands and heaved her shoulders in torment. At the decisive moment, she showed her face and closed her eyes, puckered her lips, made her eyelids twitch, and faltered with each coming breath, waiting for my kiss. When I leaned out for a casual peck, "Misao" tilted her head, clasped her hands around my neck, and sucked my lips profoundly. Then Kayo looked me in the eye.

"So young and pure, right? Who's she think she's fooling?"

We both laughed.

It occurred to me that tomorrow I was turning twenty-four.

"You send out invitations yet?" My college buddies had been bugging me to throw a birthday party, as an excuse to get the gang together. To shut them up, we were asking ten of them over for dinner.

"Of course. Everyone's already said yes. It seems like your mother's gotten a head start on the cooking, too. But tomorrow's another long day for you. You might not make it home."

"Yeah, I know."

I knew it all too well.

By the next afternoon, it was clear that we

would probably be shooting well into the night, but I didn't ask Kayo to call my mother and say that we'd be late. If anticipating my arrival was a part of the festivities, then surely my absence was part of the feast. That's right. It's better for a star to be completely absent. No matter how serious the obligation, a star is more of a star if he never arrives. Absence is his forte. The question of whether he'll show up gives the event a ceaseless undercurrent of suspense. But a true star never arrives. Showing up is for second-rate actors who need to seek attention. Tonight I'd come home to find the table heaped with dirty plates, a sign that everyone had gone home satisfied, and then I'd climb the stairs and fall asleep.

The people wait for me, checking their watches, standing at their doorsteps, but I am a speeding car that never stops. I'm huge, shiny, and new, coming from the other side of midnight. My gliding mass is strangely solid for a phantom, clad in a metal that's lighter than air. Vaulting from the abyss of my garage, deep in the deepest folds of night, I blast forth, almost floating off the ground, and rattle the sky with a crash of silver. Trees damp with dew sag and weep as I race past them, and the nocturnal birds flocking after me lay screaming in my wake. One by one, I overturn the traffic signs that line the road like white memorials. The gas stations I pass erupt in flames, leaving pocks of fire on the expanse of night … I ride and ride and never arrive.

Something strange happened that night during filming, an unlikely tragedy that did not feel like an accident. It was the perfect birthday present.

Takahama moved us into Studio 3. The space was packed wall-to-wall with scenery for the edge of town.

We were filming Scene 65, Shot 9.

Neriko Fukai was playing a seamstress from a local dress shop. Her brother, a gangster, was murdered. Neriko hates everything about the yakuza. Her brother was like a brother to me, too, and when I get out of jail and hear about his death I vow to take revenge. The scene before this, where Neriko finds me walking home from jail and breaks the news to me, is the one we shot out by the tracks.

I ask Neriko for help, but her disavowal of the

yakuza makes her want no part in the revenge. Before long, I fall in love with her. She rebuffs my numerous advances—she's had enough of the yakuza, myself included. But deep inside, I know she loves me, too, and only pushes me away because she fears my passion is a calculated step in my revenge.

Once I confirm the whereabouts of my enemy, I resolve to take him down alone. I stop by Neriko's dress shop to say goodbye. She's busy tidying up before closing. I lean in for a goodbye kiss, but she puts up a fight. If I want to die so badly, she says, I should go ahead and die already. She kicks me out. With a knife in my waistband, I leave to face my death. Neriko rushes out to stop me but I don't look back. Scene 65, Shot 9 opens with the camera behind me as I'm heading off into the night.

There are too many movies like this to count. From this snippet alone you probably get the feeling that you've seen this one a couple times at least. But there's something timeless about the mediocrity of the story, no matter how many times I find myself inside it. The yakuza with his simplistic attitude toward death and the pretty woman who resists him, hiding her true feelings, are bearers of a special kind of vulgar, trifling poetry. A hidden poetry that will be lost if any mediocrity is shed. Genius is a casualty. The poetry must never be conspicuous—its scent is only detectable when subtle. What makes the majority of these films so great is that they're shot in a way that overlooks the poetry entirely.

In the pale light of midnight's foggy street,
I'm haunted by the goodbye in your eyes.

Who would ever notice that this cheap and tired lyric has terms so rigid not a single word could be replaced? People permit its existence because they think it's harmless and derivative, with the lifespan of a mayfly, but in fact it's the only thing that's certain to survive. Just as evil never dies, neither does the sentimental. Like suckerfish clinging to the belly of a shark, threads of permanence cling to the underbelly of all formulaic poetry. It comes as a false shadow, the refuse of originality, the body dragged around by genius. It's the light that flashes from a tin roof with a tawdry grace. A tragic swiftness only the superficial can possess.

That elaborate beauty and pathos offered only by an undiscerning soul. A crude confession, like a sunset that backlights clumsy silhouettes. I love any story guarded by these principles, with this poetry at its core.

When the film starts rolling, I'll open the curtained door of the dress shop and look over my shoulder to this girl I may never see again. As I lean into the doorframe, I look out upon the neon of the empty street. This, too, perhaps for the last time. Touching the handle of the knife in my jacket, I walk out into the town.

The camera was behind me. The test run had been quick, a matter of adjusting how I prop my hand against the doorframe.

"Action!"

The clapper snapped and the buzzer rang. Despite the mass of people present, you could feel the silence ripple through the set.

Unreal time resumed its flow. I was stripped bare—deep inside a dream.

I cast a parting glance at the girl and leaned into

the doorframe, with my back turned to the camera. For a time it films my back in silence, capturing the scenery of night. Once I walk out the door, the camera will slide along a wooden rail and follow me down into the street.

With my back squarely to the lens, an uncanny landscape spread before me.

It was unlike anything I'd ever expected. A normal town at night, but through the eyes of a man who had resolved to die. What town it was, I couldn't say. I had no idea where it had come from. All I knew was that these were the lights of someplace special, someplace dear to me. They had to be.

The town was still, no one in sight. I faced three forking alleys. Willows drooped; neon signs glowed high and low across the cramped façades. Light spilled from the window of a garret apartment, of all places. Red neon gently strobed the half-torn movie posters on the telephone poles.

The neon signs flashed out of sync, and the jumbo lanterns outside the bars hung still. The doors to the bars were conspicuously dark and snugly shut. Through the glass doors of the cafes, the shadows of potted rubber trees loomed across the walls. In the window of a townhouse, mostly blocked by a partition, I spotted a red cloth covering a mirror.

What had made this town so quiet? And what had made these people hold their breath? They must have resigned themselves to the blinking of neon, the green light that the letters "LIDO" cast from the second floor of the neighboring building into the shadows of their eaves. What had left the ominous grime on the glass storefront of the realtor, papered from the inside with flyers for apartments? And what had set the door askew at such a subtle, damning angle?

The piercing fidelity of the landscape must have meant that I was watching from the gates of death. What I saw was as comprehensive as a memory, poor and wretched as a memory, as quiet, as fluorescent. I was putting it together in the way you would before you die, a last attempt to connect the life flashing before you with an acute vision of the future. I let the neon wash over me, knowing this was something I could never see again. I was no longer on a set, but in an undeniable reality, a layer within the strata of my memory.

In my short career in film, I'd never felt anything like this. Not once had I been able to completely forget that a cityscape was hollow—all façades and make-believe.

I stroked the knife in my jacket, left the dress shop, and stepped out into the town. The camera followed, soundless down the wooden rail. It was nothing short of a miracle that I'd stepped into this textured landscape, a living version of memory. It may sound contradictory, but it felt like I had stepped into a painting on the wall and was standing, dumbfounded, inside its panorama.

As I walked along, it became impossible to deny that these empty streets would eventually open onto sprawling tracks where trains came rushing in and out of town, extending naturally to a grand city, and a harbor, and beyond the sea to other countries with their own cities and harbors.

When this strange suggestion of reality bumped up against unquestionable proof, I couldn't believe my eyes: the black door of the nearest bar swung open, and before me stood a beautiful young woman in a periwinkle cocktail dress.

In the flow of unreal time, I expect things to proceed as planned. The future is fixed; I know its every detail and can see the route ahead of me, like a car negotiating a winding slope. This girl was not part of the plan.

She stood in the shadow of the doorway, smiling brightly. Her skin looked awfully pale. It could have been her makeup, or the neon washing over us. Her nose and eyebrows were obscured; only her sad eyes and tiny lips were clearly defined. All I could see of her petite and slender body was where her cleavage met her dress. Her black hair blended with the darkness of the eaves. I completely forgot about acting and fell head over heels in love with this mysterious beauty.

Her arrival made the town's sense of reality complete. I was convinced that I had slipped into another dimension, an actual place—all of it was real! The neon, the lanterns, the signboards, the willows, the telephone poles, and the glass door of the realtor. I'd been imagining they were all artificial, but now I was awake. I was positive that in about ten hours the sun would sweep the landscape, a newborn sun rising between the hunkered roofs.

She came toward me, arms outstretched, and in a strident, forlorn voice called out my name.

"Richie! Richie Mizuno!"

My real name. Not the name of my role. Her arms slapped my sides and closed around me in a bear hug.

A grenade of vitriol went off behind us.

"Cut!" screamed Takahama.

Everyone looked furious. Soon the entire cast was visible, peeking from the scenery. One guy threw open the glass door of the realtor. Another jumped out of a low window. The faces of the lighting crew poked out from the catwalks in the ceiling.

Kayo rushed over to my side.

The assistant director started screaming.

"What's going on here—who the hell are you? Thanks to you, everybody's gone nuts." He grabbed at the bosom of the girl's cocktail dress. She shrieked but couldn't speak.

*

The grumblings of the veteran actors helped clarify the situation. This girl was a "new face" who had joined the studio a year ago. In her impatience to land a decent role, she ran herself ragged and wound up with some kind of an infection that led to a nervous breakdown. Desperate, she concluded that the only way to make it was to pull some bizarre stunt, anything to appear alongside none other than yours truly—and she was ready to resort to measures no sane actor would chance.

But this incident didn't follow the usual course of events, with her removal from the set. What happened next was comical, all too typical of the film industry, and it sickens me just thinking about it. Takahama's anger didn't last. As he looked into the new girl's eyes, he felt a gust of inspiration.

He wrote her into the scene as a crazy girl who jumps inexplicably in front of me, embraces me, and refuses to let go. Meanwhile, Neriko, who has been watching from the dress shop, is spurred by jealousy and rushes up to pull me away.

"Doesn't that turn it into a comedy?" the assistant director asked.

Takahama responded with a glare. That settled things.

"What's your name?" the director finally asked.

"Yuri Asano."

Yuri had landed an unbelievable role, and the stable of actors—who despite waiting all day had not even been cast as extras—observed this injustice with icy stares. They dispersed, muttering nonsense about how unfair it was.

We jumped headfirst into the test run.

Yuri was petrified and tightened up. Her arms and legs were stiff, as if caught in plaster. I absorbed the icy glares they cast upon this actress who had overstepped her bounds. Yuri's body would not regain the fluid liberty of that moment. That sense of living realness, felt only once, was gone for good. The sentiment had shriveled up. Her body was clammy, quaking from her center, her feet unsteady, unable to move even a few steps.

We kept trying, but anyone could see that it was over. Takahama heaved a sigh and announced that Yuri was no longer needed. We were returning to the original plan. When the casting director, whose job it was to pick our roles, heard Takahama make this announcement he rushed onto the set after the producer.

During Yuri's impromptu audition, the casting director's reaction had been so palpable I could almost hold it in my hands. His face was saying, "Here we go. If she pulls this off it's gonna be a disaster."

But to his relief, Yuri couldn't pull it off, and like a pair of detectives, he and the producer escorted her off set. It drained the last of the blood from her face. She looked back, as if to say goodbye, but I didn't even bother to return her glance.

The producer resolved to cut her on the spot. Nevertheless, she lingered in the greenroom, refusing to go home.

Shooting ended around ten. I went out back and found the other actors in a state of panic. Yuri had snuck into one of the starlet's dressing rooms and overdosed.

Still wearing my costume and makeup, I charged over to her. Kayo, who loves this sort of chaos, had beat me there.

Yuri was doped up on Valamin. A group of actors laid her out on a bench and waited for the doctor to arrive.

Her eyes were closed, but the thickness of her makeup kept her from looking like she was really on the verge of death. The men gathered around her pliant body, and even those who'd spent the day fighting each other now seemed congenial in the presence of this dying girl, as if her body were exuding sensuality.

When the doctor arrived with a nurse, the producer asked him the most obvious question:

"Is she going to make it?"

The young doctor pulled back one of her eyelids and checked her pulse.

"She'll make it," he stated.

We gave the doctor space, assuming he was going to have to pump her stomach.

"I'm going to give her an injection. I'll need you gentlemen to hold her down. She's not going to like this."

The men exchanged obscene glances and giggles. A group of them went over and held Yuri by the wrists and ankles.

The doctor drove a shot of saline into her left arm. Soon she began to writhe, like a snake working its skin free. We watched the twitches grow more violent. An anguished voice escaped her throat.

"It … it hurts!"

Kayo looked my way and for an instant let a smirk show at the corner of her mouth. But just as soon, as if forgetting I was there, she turned to watch the body of the girl revive.

Yuri's chest arched sharply, her breasts threatening to burst from her dress. Her left arm snapped free, slapping the syringe out of the doctor's hand.

"Hold her down, get that wrist."

An actor in a windbreaker knelt by Yuri and pinned her arm down. The fury of her shoulders revealed the outrage of her muscle.

Each time she sent the syringe flying, she squealed "It hurts! It hurts!" at a higher and raspier pitch. It was all so natural. Having shaken off the stiffness that had temporarily constrained her on set, she reclaimed the natural presence of her first appearance. It was as if the overdose was not about her death at all, but the death of the woman who had been so rigid during the test run. Eventually the doctor grew impatient and slipped the tip of the syringe into a vein on the back of her delicate hand. She had a silver manicure. Absorbing the injection, the thin layer of muscle under her skin convulsed. A ribbon of blood dribbled from the needle. Her voice grew shriller still. The yells were real. She gritted her clean, straight teeth. All eyes were on Yuri! Her expression was shameless, every inch of her exposed. But with her return to consciousness, she found herself back in the disgraces of this bright and garish world.

Kayo's eyes were twinkling. With her lips parted to reveal her silver teeth, she stared on drunkenly as Yuri's body jerked with life.

That night, back in my bedroom, Kayo did something awful that the average person would never allow. But I was fine with it and did more than just allow it.

"Yuri Asano, right? She's pretty. Too pretty to make it as a star."

Lying faceup in the dim light, Kayo said those

last few words like she was singing me a song.

"Hey watch this. Watch for a sec."

I sat up from the sofa to see what she would do.

Kayo closed her eyes and made herself uncomfortably rigid. A thin screech, like a baby pigeon's, left her lips. Her voice grew louder and clearer, and as the words "It hurts" took shape, what began as subtle twitches swelled into waves of energy. She screamed "It hurts!" and thrashed her arm through the air. Her silver teeth glimmered when she squealed. To me it looked like she was laughing, and eventually she did.

"It hurts! It hurts!"

She whipped her hair and clawed at her breasts with a passion that was almost sacrificial. The laughter driving the performance spun out of control.

"… Oh my god! … Oh my god!"

Kayo sat up, convulsing with laughter, only to fall back flat and start in with "It hurts! It hurts!" again.

There's something about Kayo in these fits of delirium that shoots me through the heart. At times like these, she's truly at her best. Every move she makes is resolute, a vow to resist the pull of tragedy, to poke fun at every situation, no matter how painful or grave, like someone flicking a watermelon to hear the sound it makes before they buy it. Her laughter was potent enough to scorch the grass for miles around, to putrefy a field of ripe red strawberries.

Watching Kayo sucked me in. I jumped on top of her, laughing so hard I almost cried. She screamed "Get off of me!" but I refused and sprawled over her convulsing body. Her laughter spattered at my chest like oil roaring in a pan.

By the next morning, the PR Office had reworked the story of attempted suicide into a pure romance. A minor actress, so blinded by her love for me she couldn't keep herself off of the set, chose to take her own life rather than live a lifetime without me, but thanks to my intervention she was spared. To preserve the beauty of this memory, she had given up acting for good. They'd even written a response for me to read when the reporters asked about what happened.

"Of course I never saw her before. I was simply overcome with a sense of duty, as her colleague, to do anything I could to save her life. If you saw a woman drowning in the water, would you make sure she was beautiful before diving in to save her?"

3

It's useless trying to explain what it feels like in the spotlight. The very thing that makes a star spectacular is the same thing that strikes him from the world at large and makes him an outsider.

I forgot almost everything about Yuri Asano's attempted suicide, but over and over, frame by frame, my mind replayed her gestures and the faces that she made when they revived her with the saline. The Yuri who jumped in front of the camera still stood in the shadows, but the Yuri who screamed "It hurts! It hurts!" and flailed her limbs lay wholly, incandescently before me.

Her success was absolute—a success no one could contest. The men were sweating. Holding down her mighty limbs, they watched the flesh of her white thighs twitch and recoil under their weight. The other men gathered around and took in every detail, from the flaring of her nostrils to the flash of her tongue between her parted lips. As if it were their duty, as if following an order, they watched her from all sides.

The position of her body made the spectacle supreme. With her eyes firmly shut, fake eyelashes and all, and undistracted by her senses, Yuri was submerged. That's right. Her mind was underwater. Her senses had been caught in the blurred grayness at the bottom of the sea, but her body had made it to the surface, its every curve and crevice bathed in the violent light. When Yuri yelled "It hurts!" her voice was aimed at the abyss. This was not a cry out into the world, and certainly not a message. It was a frank display of physicality, expressed through pure presence and pure flesh, unburdened by the weight of consciousness.

I wanted to study her, to watch her do it all over again. She had managed to attain the sublime state that actors always dream of. That two-bit actress had really pulled it off... without even knowing she had done it.

Among yesterday's fan letters was a painstaking confession from a teenage girl, who wrote to say she used a photograph of me each night to masturbate. Kayo read every word of it aloud.

Listening from the sofa, I imagined the girl's changing body.

Alone in her room, completely out of sight, she wove her hand between her legs, her thin fingers like a deft and agile comb. Her handiwork was pointless, harmless, lovable, and ladylike. Her fingers were precise, their motions practiced. She was the figure of rapture, and the cloth she wove so small, no wider than a handkerchief.

But the girl was anything but dreaming. She wove her cloth with steady focus and fastidious attention.

Nobody was watching. There was no way my

photograph was looking back at her. But there I was, under her voracious gaze!

Through this sort of exchange, a man and woman can consummate a pure and timeless intimacy without ever actually meeting. In some deserted square, in the middle of a sunny day—it would manifest and consummate, without either of us ever knowing.

Given the choice, I'd much rather have a girl masturbating somewhere to my picture than actually trying to sleep with me. Real love always plays out at a distance.

Despite billing the film as a grand production shot in lifelike color on Cinemascope, the studio only gave us twenty-five days to shoot, forcing us as usual to move at a grueling pace, working each day late into the night. Every morning I woke before seven, headed to the set, and didn't come home till past eleven. But that wasn't the end of it. To film the night scenes on location, we sometimes worked until dawn three nights in a row. All the while there were heaps of conversations, photo shoots, and interviews for magazines. The PR Office scheduled meetings with the newspapers during my lunch breaks. I barely had a chance to chew my food, much less taste it. The other day I looked down and saw red in the toilet bowl, but didn't tell a soul.

I was outside, pacing in the brutal sunlight while they were switching out the sets, when the producer clapped me on the shoulder.

"Your name's getting bigger and bigger, kid. Pretty soon we're gonna have to get you doing one a month."

"Great. I can't wait."

"Whenever the president goes out to have some fun, he always takes along a few photographs of you to hand out to the geisha girls, to see how they react. In his mind, geisha are the most self-centered and honest type of girl. 'A geisha never lies.' That's his motto. Could be worse. But listen to this. When he pulls out the photos of you, the girls fight over who gets to keep them. He said it makes him feel like Mr. Moneybags, throwing coins into a crowd."

"You don't say."

"I guess the geisha got pretty worked up last time."

The producer was an amicably cynical man, but it wasn't until recently that he'd begun to speak with me this casually.

It was strange to have a day this clear. The rainy season had come early, with almost daily showers since the start of May. Lucky for us, we were done with most of the location shooting. Inside, the studio was unbelievably humid, the air thick with a promise of mold.

Here's how things progress after the scene I mentioned earlier, where I head out to confront my enemy in the face of certain death. Keep in mind that some of the later scenes had actually already been filmed, to accommodate the schedules of certain members of the cast: I bid farewell to Neriko and leave the dress shop. Off into the city lights, as if we'll never meet again. Once she's alone, Neriko finally realizes how much she loves me. She runs out after me, grabs ahold of me, confesses her love, and tries to get me to abandon my mission. Eventually I give in and put it off for one more day, to spend the night with Neriko in our first "passionate embrace." Things get pretty hot and heavy.

Trouble is, the next morning, the guy dies anyway, in a car accident. You'd think I'd be relieved to hear he died without my intervention—Neriko sure thought so—but instead I resent her for stripping me of my life's purpose. After just one night together, I toss Neriko aside and set my sights on the runaway girls who hang around Ueno Station. I lure them in, set them up as streetwalkers, and make a living as their manager. That's where Neriko finds me.

On this particular morning, the scene was set in a dingy hotel room in Ueno, where I've taken one of the runaways to bed. Everyone was saying that these next fifteen shots could take all afternoon.

Ken, the wizard of the lighting crew, was sure of it.

"It's our first day on set. No matter how fast he tries to go there's no way we're finishing this morning."

Takahama liked filming out of order. Say, for example, the camera setup is the same for Shot 5, Shot 8, and Shot 10 of a given scene. His method is to shoot all three in quick succession, out of sequence. In a pinch, he has no qualms about burning through shots from completely different sections of the movie. If Scene 60, Shot 5 and Scene 75, Shot 5 use the same setup, he shoots them back-to-back. When the cast for the scenes is identical, the effect can disorient the uninitiated. Without actually going anywhere, you hop into a time machine and blast into the future, then back into the past, then back to the future, forced all the while to keep track of where you are in the script.

Habitually deferring to efficiency and economy can make life start to seem less consequential. Let's say somebody's just cut me up and I'm in serious pain. In the next shot, without moving an inch, I'm miraculously healed, but in the shot after that, I'll have to start wincing again from the freshness of the wound.

If you get too used to living life this way, the steady flow of real time—where there is no turning back—begins to feel boring and stale. Let's say I meet a girl. I want to skip ahead to when we're sleeping together, but I can't, which makes me antsy, and it feels absurd that I can't jump ahead to where I'm sick of her, or back to the freedom that I had before we met.

I recall a rare afternoon off: I went shopping on the Ginza, where I witnessed a man being arrested for stealing a pair of cufflinks, under the cover of the crowd gathered there to see me. It felt like we were in a dream: a star and a shoplifter is each a rare encounter, but seeing us together cracked the superstructure of reality. Everyone was watching. The shoplifter was a grungy middle-aged man, and at the time I was still twenty-three, a burning beacon of youth. When they arrested him, the crowd cheered and our eyes met. His face was in agony.

At that moment, it felt like this middle-aged man and I were pulled loose from reality, from the gleaming store displays, from the racks lined with shirts of every color, from the uproar of the crowd. Like a rose being plucked down to its stem, the world tore back before my eyes and showed me its interior. It felt like we were in a scene being shot out of order, at the mercy of some unseen director.

That shoplifter was me, only twenty years older! The moment he reached out to touch those handsome cufflinks with their precious stones, reality began to slip away, and he and I switched places. The next shot in the scene was rolling, only he was playing me.

"Please forgive us for all the excitement," the store manager begged me, once the shoplifter had been apprehended and taken away. "There's such a crowd today that I'm afraid you won't be able to have a proper look around. Why not make yourself comfortable upstairs? It's a bit of a mess, but at least up there you can take your time and look things over."

We walked through towers of cardboard boxes and up a steep and narrow staircase to a disorderly office area on the second floor, where I was offered a chair. Since I'd come to find a necktie, the manager personally fetched me a selection of skinny club ties from America, Germany, and Italy. A girl from the shop brought tea and asked me for an autograph. I signed her piece of paper and she slinked off. The manager told me to take my time and disappeared, leaving me alone with my decision.

Up there in the office, the bustle of Ginza kept its distance, and the music and the people dancing at the neighboring cabaret, separated only by a window, felt like they were in another world. I was alone, my head cocked staring at a mirror on the wall—if there's a mirror in the room, I notice it right away and answer its passionate gaze. In that messy little room, it was like the ratty burlap sack of Ginza had been emptied inside out.

Again I felt the strange sensation of filming out of order. I stroked the fabric of a German tie in an elegant silvery gray and ran its length between my fingers ... through the mirror, head still cocked, I took a careful look around the room.

But when I heard the manager climbing the stairs, I pulled the necktie from my pocket and carefully returned it to its box. Even if I'd really stolen it, no one would have labeled me a thief. The manager would merely have sent along an invoice and had a blast telling his friends about the funny trick I'd played.

Three rookie actresses—Aiko, Baba, and Chie—stood around me, dressed up in fancy outfits that gave them away as country girls too far from home.

Soon each of them would "taste my venom." They were trembling, eyes fixed on their scripts, no time to listen to the jokes I made.

When me and the first one, Aiko, were called to the lofted upper level of the set, Aiko almost lost her footing on the shoddy ladder.

"Hey babe, watch your step!" Ken said, touching her hips as if to catch her. "Tokyo is a dangerous place."

The lighting crew always perked up for the bedroom scenes. You could hear them joking all around us, eyes peeled.

Takahama talked us through the scene.

"You two are sitting on the futon. Richie takes Aiko in his arms, but she jerks away, backs up against the wall, and says her line. Richie isn't fazed and throws her down. Aiko lays on the futon crying. Watching her cry, Richie stands, casually undoes his tie, and takes his shirt off. Then he says his line. That's it. Got it? Aiko puts up a front, but she's already thrown open the castle gates. Alright. Lights!"

Aiko couldn't get her part right, so we kept starting over. The clapper snapped and snapped. Working patiently beside her through take after take gave me a chance to reevaluate my own performance. I realized that when I tugged off the tie, I could wrap one end of it around my finger and fling the whole thing like a streamer through the air. I tried this out during the third test run and Takahama didn't comment, meaning he approved.

"Hey, Kayo, grab my mints," I yelled down to the lower level between takes. Kayo sat in a chair with the script open in her lap, quietly knitting her turquoise sweater, avoiding the banter between the set photographer and the guys from PR.

When people saw the sweater, they gave her a hard time, asking "Who's the present for?" Kayo was ready with an evil eye and would tell them, deadpan, "It's for me. Yarn's cheap in bulk this time of year."

From the upper level of the set, that turquoise sweater made a cheery blemish in the cloying blackness of the floor, which twinkled wet from everyone's umbrellas.

Kayo knit the sweater sloppily on purpose. She made it fit wrong on her body, in a blousy shape long out of style. Knowing her, at some point later in the year, once everyone had forgotten all about her summer knitting project, she'd show up in the sweater and crouch down at the back of the studio, waiting to overhear their whispered laughter.

Because I knew what she was up to, that half-finished turquoise sweater seemed to me, from my vantage in the loft, like the very hue of her nefarious intentions.

This was apt knitting for summer. Her fingers maneuvered through the heart of it, as if secretly laboring to humiliate every worldly convention that the climate and the seasons had to offer.

But most of all this patch of turquoise yarn in the darkest corner of the set was a thing of beauty, like a virgin spring, a calm collection of her artifice.

I like to have a mint before I film a kissing scene. Kayo always had them at the ready, and I got a kick out of seeing the face she made when she came running with them in her hand.

That face was her strength. No matter how prickly the circumstance, she remained stern and officious, without a trace of jealousy. I loved seeing her this way.

Kayo sped to the top of the ladder, legs pumping in those cheap black slacks, and handed me the case of silver mints. It was small enough that I could easily have kept it in my pocket, but it was my policy not to spoil the crisp lines of my clothes with even the smallest object. The slimmest prop could compromise the way the cloth fell or the way I moved, and when I gestured passionately the mics could catch the mints rattling in their case.

I assumed a stoic air, knotted my tie, rolled up my sleeves, and shook a few mints into my palm. Against my skin, these prosaic pellets felt like currency, little symbols of the kisses I relied on for my livelihood.

But the scene we were filming had no kiss. I was giving Kayo a hard time

"Actually, I'm kind of thirsty."

"Why didn't you just say so then? I'll get some tea."

With a glare that cut right through my mischief, Kayo's eyes, for just an instant, seemed to harbor a faint resentment—the type of look that she learned to hide so well when we were filming. I thought it was funny.

"It's fine. But let's have tea next time. The two of us," I said. I even winked.

Just then Ken walked by.

"Hubba hubba! Tea for two."

We cut that one a little too close.

When the director shouted "Ready?" Aiko was already on the verge of tears. The lighting crew, who had been leering at us through the test run of the bedroom scene, burst into action and screeched commands. They rushed to adjust the lighting, to make sure that the shadow of the boom mic dangling from its bamboo pole didn't drop into the frame, and that none of the lights dispelled the fantasy of the hotel room's lone bulb by casting a layered shadow on the wall.

This restlessness before the main event was like the thrill you get from hearing circus animals stomp the earth before they march into the ring.

"Lights: you ready?" Takahama asked. "Let me guess—you need a minute."

He spoke sarcastically to hide his annoyance, but no one was going to laugh at a joke so clumsy and barbed.

Under the lights, dust kicked up from the corners of the set glinted and danced like flecks of gold. Kayo came over silently and held the tiny mirror before me. I took a quick peek and was pleased with the condition of my makeup. For a second I practiced the expression I was supposed to make when the camera cuts to me.

Hanging on the hotel wall were tacky signs advertising "naptime" for 200 yen and an overnight stay, breakfast included, for 700. Beside the signs there were dirty poems written on tall strips of paper. A traditional doll of a woman carrying a basket used for making salt stood in a little alcove at the edge of the tatami floor. The cramped space— only three tatami mats—was lined with red and blue embroidered satin pillows.

Conscious of her inexperience, Aiko bowed and said she'd follow my lead. Her calico dress had too many pleats and a sweeping hem, like something a country girl had copied from a fashion magazine. But she was far from petit, and it suited her pastoral figure perfectly. Staring off into space, her plump arms bare, she drew shapes on the tatami with her fingers and practiced her one line to herself over and over. I hate witnessing ambition, even in a woman. I had to look away.

"Action!" Takahama wailed.

The assistant director flashed and snapped a clapper with SCENE 71, SHOT 3 written on it in chalk. The buzzer rang, and the stream of artificial time gushed forth.

I took Aiko in my arms. In my embrace, her body quivered like a bowl of pudding. She was supposed to be writhing, but she wasn't using enough force. I had to overcompensate and throw my hands back to make it look like she had flung me off. She bumped her back against the wall.

She was supposed to say—

"No, no! Stay away from me!"

—but instead said:

"No, no! Stay with me!"

"Cut!" the director yelled. "Cut! You've got it ass-backwards. Come on! I'll cut you slack during the test runs, but once we're using film, you're accountable. Film ain't free."

"I'm sorry!"

Aiko's voice was shaky, but I didn't feel particularly sympathetic. When it was someone else's fault, I breathed easy and sided with the director. Takahama's displeasure could sometimes verge on the majestic. He towered over this trembling amateur actress, drowning her out like the crash of a symphony. Slip-ups like these, blunders that ruin a take, seemed to make him feel like the glass castle he was laboring to construct was shattering to pieces. He planned his scenes shot by shot, like a criminal plotting out the perfect crime. When he hit some obstacle along the way—a mouse, for instance, kicking a tin can off of a shelf onto the floor—he would reject this unsolicited detail, however realistic, as his sworn enemy.

I loved watching the agonized expression that came over Takahama's face when he had to throw a scene because an actor flubbed a line or made the wrong expression: it was the grimace of swallowing the bitter reality of incompetence. And ruined celluloid.

"Alright. Action!"

The clapper snapped and the buzzer rang. Silence rippled through the set.

When I cradled Aiko in my arms, she flung my hands away and threw herself decisively against the wall, whipping back her pale jaw. The shock made her nod mechanically, like a doll someone had tossed. Her teeth clacked like ceramic.

"No, no! Stay away from me!"

I was sitting with my feet free, ready to stand, before she'd even spoken. I sprang up flawlessly and towered over her. The camera shot us from the side, filming Aiko's trembling face as she watched me with an expression that the script described as "full of fear and anticipation."

I turned toward the camera and dropped my hands onto her shoulders, to push her down. Aiko was too stiff and didn't understand how to go down gracefully. It felt like I was yanking on the handle of a creaky pump that badly needed greasing. But I had to make my movements fluid, effortless, and strong.

Once Aiko had fallen to the bed and started crying (though in a way that left much to be desired), I took center stage. Finally, I was able to move without resistance.

I looked down at the crying woman at my feet and smirked. She arched her back, pushing her chest out just enough to accentuate her breasts. I twisted up my lips, shiny with lip balm, ran my fingers through my hair, and tugged apart the tie, in the rakish way I'd worked out during the test run.

I took care not to rush, loosening the knot in three deliberate motions, each gesture dripping with my readiness to enjoy this woman's body.

But I had to keep from appearing to be a villain. A heartthrob must always be supple; his face must never lose its natural innocence. I ripped open my shirt, nearly popping off the buttons. The amber muscles of my chest, prepped earlier with body makeup, gleamed lustrously before the camera.

I freed my arms from my sleeves and delivered my line: "Quit crying. You know I'm gonna treat you right."

"Cut!"

Takahama took a sharp breath. In the usual sulking way, he let out his reluctant signal of approval.

"OK."

4

It's become a tradition for me to pin up the life-size poster from my current project right inside the front door. Every night, when I get home, I'm the first one there to greet me.

As we neared the end of filming, the posters kept coming. That night, I found the life-size color poster of me waiting in the mail. The format was always the same: I stood alone against a white background. Theaters everywhere would paste these onto sheets of plywood, cut around my body with a jigsaw, and stand me up outside the entrance. On windy days, there was nothing worse than passing a movie theater on the edge of town and seeing myself knocked facedown on the pavement.

On this particular poster, I wore the standard suit, but with a crimson polo shirt under the jacket. The neck of the shirt was open, and a solid gold pendant of a skull was glinting from my chest. This composition was yet another masterpiece from our set photographer. He'd really made it come alive by shooting from a low angle, to make me taller. The PR Office had been picky about the face I made and asked for subtle adjustments until finally giving this one their approval. My cheeks were rosy, my smile sober.

Coming home exhausted late at night to find this cheery character waiting gave me a boost of energy, because I knew that when we took that photograph I was equally exhausted—my carefree grin a total lie.

The next morning, the house was blanketed in fog. I was standing out front, annoyed that my taxi was running late, when a group of schoolgirls emerged from the fog and started pinching at my thighs. I heard myself shriek, and in that instant the white trim on the backflaps of their sailor suits vanished into the mist.

That day we were supposed to shoot the final scene at Shinobazu Pond in Ueno Park, but the foul weather made us stay on set for two more days, until it cleared and we could finally head out on location. Here, Neriko, in a last-ditch effort to convince me to leave the yakuza, drags me to a bench by the edge of the pond and confesses her deepest secret, which I never saw coming: her brother was the reason I wound up in jail. He was my role model, my idol—and the one who talked. The guys who killed him had their own agenda, but unbeknownst to them, they'd settled my score.

I shake my head at the stupidity of this world of crime. Taken by Neriko's emotional sincerity, I help her into a rowboat and paddle us out into the pond. She offers me a piece of gum, which I refuse; she insists, and finally I accept it and proceed to chew the gum with a huge grin on my face. "THE

END" floats up from the surface of the water and begins to grow, but in the foreground, back at the water's edge, you see the figure of a plainclothes cop cupping the photo of me that the precinct circulated when they billed me as a pimp. As he sizes up our little boat, the black back of his jacket swells like a thundercloud to fill the screen as "THE END" peaks in size, and the movie ends. I thought this philosophical comment on the fleeting nature of contentment wasn't such a bad way to wind things up. It was a message that appealed to the lucky and the unlucky alike.

At lunchtime on the day we shot the pond scene, a film columnist from a classy women's magazine met us at a sushi bar in Ueno to hold an interview. Squeezing through the throngs of fans peeking through the windows, she joined us at the counter, taking her seat with an obvious air of education. When she was finished with her questions, she peered at me through her glasses, sighed, and said, "I feel bad for you. I really do."

Plenty of stars would fall for this sort of line— they're tired of being simply adored or envied and are quick to take a sign of sympathy as proof of being understood. Not me. All she would get from me was a naive young celebrity, complacent with his fame. When she stood up to go, Kayo, who'd been eating sushi beside me, started coughing in the most believable way, and sent two or three beads of rice flying at the woman's back.

The studio kept things moving and was already abuzz with preparations for the next production. As soon as things are wrapping up, you dive right in again.

The next movie was a romantic tragedy set in high society. Once we were finished shooting at the pond that evening, the producer, thinking I could learn a thing or two about the upper crust, took me along to a fancy party. The gathering was hosted by a former prince at his former palace, now a hotel, where once a month he held gatherings for the families of the former nobility and those of solid pedigree.

When we arrived, the producer carted me around making introductions and schmoozing with everyone we met. I'd never had so many people fail to recognize me—somehow no one knew my name, and the elegant young ladies claimed they'd never seen my films. The second we were introduced, they resumed their conversations.

On the ride home, the producer was suddenly a champion for the common man.

"Oh how the mighty have fallen! On a normal night at home those assholes are probably roasting herring on sticks around a fire pit. Anyway, it doesn't matter. Movies are about the make-believe. Forget about imitating anyone or anything. Just give us a pure, gallant young gentleman, okay?"

As I sat through his pep talk, my mind drifted back to a moment at the party when the producer had introduced me to one of the beautiful young women without mentioning my profession. She'd tilted her neck ever so slightly as she looked me over. This was a breach of manners, no matter how you saw it. If she really didn't know my name, custom would have kept her from betraying it with such a gesture. Tilting her neck like that, so elegantly you could almost miss it. She knew what she was doing. Her features were chilly and refined; she had the trim nose and flat brow of an antique doll, and her little red lips looked like a spot of red ink left by a dropper.

"Maybe she's just being coquettish," I thought. "The neck thing is just a tease."

But I wasn't going to fall for it. I bet she thought pretending that she'd never heard of me was certain to entice me. Most stars would take the bait. Not me. If she didn't recognize my face or know my name, I didn't exist, at least not to her—but a girl has to be pretty damn arrogant to try and seduce you by denying your existence, and I'm not some dreamer who would chase a girl like that, since I meant nothing to her. Maybe Kayo really was the only one for me.

After filming the last scene, our days were spent taking care of little bits and pieces and dubbing in the dialog. All the serious dramatic work was done. We shot all seven of the remaining phone call scenes in just one day. I grew weary of holding the receiver, and tired of the clever ways that Takahama captured every phone call from a different angle. Out of pride, he refused to rely on the old standby of cutting to a close-up of the telephone as it begins to ring.

In the afternoon, I stepped out into the sun and went for a walk on the studio grounds. There was nothing to see. It may as well have been the compound of a factory. On the other side, at the building where the producer had his office, I spotted the studio's sapphire flag flapping from a pole at the peak of the roof. It must have been there all along, but this was the first time that I'd noticed it.

The flag spasmed in the breeze. Just as it would fall limp, it whipped against the sky, snapping between shadow and light, as if any moment it would tear free and fly away. I don't know why, but watching it infused me with a sadness that ran down to the deepest limits of my soul and made me think of suicide. There are so many ways to die.

By the guardhouse at the main gate, I was surrounded by another crowd of fans begging for autographs, but was so absurdly tired I could barely write my own name. Shameless fans waved their autograph books over the outstretched books of other fans, the pages piling from my chest to my chin. The hand that held its book most desperately above the others was half-consumed by a violet birthmark. Tracing the arm to its body, I discovered an oafish woman with a tiny, sour face, proudly thrusting this violet hand at me, her birthmark nearly pressed against my cheek.

I was once more overtaken by a deep fatigue; my thoughts returned to death. If I was going to die, now would be as good a time as any. Rather than a death cushioned by pleasure, I would die embracing a despicable filth. Cheek in the gutter, curled up against the corpse of a stray cat.

That night, I finally confessed to Kayo my unreasonable urge to die.

"In that case, stick your head in there and get it over with." She gestured toward the green electric fan we'd just bought to fight the heat. Its blades were metal.

"I'm not kidding," I said, staring into the handsome blur.

I was drawn to the cool whir coming from its bluish vortex. It commanded the airflow of our little room, making it feel like time was moving in the way that I know best, the artificial flow when the camera is rolling. Only there could I breathe easy, talk of death without fear, and die without suffering.

From her usual position, sitting with her legs out to the side, wearing nothing but a slip, Kayo flashed her silver teeth and gazed at me reclining on the sofa.

"Of course you're going to die. I wouldn't be the least surprised. You call it unreasonable, but you don't need a reason."

"Right. I don't need a reason," I agreed, striking a grave tone. I was stretched out on the sofa like a cadaver, my fingers interwoven at my chest.

"You're twenty-four, at the top of your game. A heartthrob. A movie star, more famous by the day. No poor relatives to take care of, in perfect health. Everything is set for you to die. If you died today, maybe everybody would forget you. Not like you're James Dean or anything, but maybe they'd love you even more, and pile so many flowers on your grave that there'd be no more room to leave them. But what difference does it make?"

"You're right. It makes none."

In the midnight air, churned by the fan, jazz streamed out of the radio like an excited swarm of golden flies. I was absurdly tired.

So tired I didn't know if I wanted to sleep or if I wanted to die.

"Listen, Rikio. It's only human that you want to die. And when you do, instead of eulogizing you, I'll write a thousand-page memoir to set the story straight. Then your 'assistant' Kayo will finally take off her mask."

"Sounds fun. I'll just sit back in my grave and watch their jaws drop."

"But Ri-ki-oh …"

Kayo sat up and crossed her bare legs. The sight of her plump thighs would have jolted anyone who'd only seen her during the day. "At least my thighs are still young," she said to herself, pinching at her skin.

"Ri-ki-oh …"

She uncrossed her legs and crawled across the floor to the sofa, where I lay in just my underwear. Leaning close, she traced a finger up my thigh. "Hah. Our thighs are the only part of us that matches."

"Get off me! I want to die!"

"Of course you do—who wouldn't, with a life like this? So go ahead and die. But listen, Rikio. It has to be an accident. Something that catches you totally off-guard. If you're thinking about dying in some fantastic blaze of your own making, forget about it. Has the 'gaze of reality' you're so fixated on finally started getting to you? Do you want to be human now like everybody else? Stop being so predictable. The real world can't wait for you to die. And maybe for me, too.... That's its plan. It wants to cleanse the planet by eradicating everything that contradicts its vision.

"Consider why you're still alive. This power you get out of 'being seen' is just a way of playing by reality's rules and doing what they ask of you. In exchange, they let us have our secret life together, our passionate artifice, and especially the faith behind the artifice, because they know that a convincing sense of reality can only be born from an unholy faith.

"For a star, being seen is everything. But the powers that be are well aware that being seen is no more than a symptom of the gaze. They know that the reality everyone thinks they see and feel draws from the spring of artifice that you and I are guarding. To keep the public pacified, the spring must always be shielded from the world by masks. And these masks are worn by stars.

"But the real world is always waiting for its stars to die. If you never cycle out the masks, you run the risk of poisoning the well. The demand for new masks is insatiable.

"If you want to stay new in the eyes of the world, do what I say. Run this mystic vein, scorn the real world, curse it with all your heart, but trust the artifice. To put it in more human terms, don't ever lift a finger. From the moment I first saw you, I knew that you could take it. I knew that you …"

That's basically what I remember hearing Kayo say, but at some point I drifted off to sleep.

5

The day after we called it a wrap was the first day the sun was harsh enough to feel like summer. It was almost like a holiday for me, but in my usual masochistic way I went to the studio early for a haircut.

Kayo had a meeting with the PR Office, and I walked clear across the studio grounds toward the old squat building that was the barber shop. The vast lawn was banded with islands of light. On the other side, next to a row of tour buses, squads of extras waited to be shuttled off-site for location shoots.

Someone gave directions through a megaphone: "All those assigned to head into the city with Director Takeuchi, please proceed to your designated bus."

The voice, grainy and barely comprehensible, repeated the directions. The extras wore the robes of vagabonds. As if on cue, the whole posse looked my way.

I plodded toward them through the sunlight. At the buses, I said "Good morning!" to Director Takeuchi, gave an affable "Good morning!" to his crew, and then turned to admire the swaths of cloud lingering over the woods edging the lot.

I was modest and merry, everybody's favorite star. Along came Ken from lighting.

"Morning, Ken!"

"Richie! You're out early. Who's the lucky lady?"

"Come off it, Ken. You see these eyes? These are the eyes of a virgin!"

I pulled my eyelids back, to prove it. We parted in front of the barber shop.

Inside, I sank into the ancient chair and watched

the bright white sheet billow up in the reflection of the mirror. As it settled over my chest, the quiet old barber picked up his scissors and went to work behind me. He knew exactly what I wanted.

The snipping of the scissors made me sleepy. Off to the side, on the seats by the sunny window, I saw the morning paper, tossed aside and pulled apart.

Since I had nothing on my mind, I thought of Kayo.

I was certain she was over at the PR Office. She had to be. But who could prove it?

Battling sleep made the pattern of my thoughts grow hazy and obscure.

If I couldn't say for sure that Kayo was at the PR Office, could I be sure that she existed? What if she wasn't actually anywhere? Not the PR Office, not the soundstage, not anywhere on the face of the earth? If Kayo was something only I could see, then why did everyone pretend to see her? Or maybe I just thought they were pretending. What if no one ever mentioned her because they couldn't actually see her?

A snipped bang dropped across my vision like

the shadow of a bird. The problem of Kayo's existence prodded my numb brain bluntly, almost imperceptibly.

If Kayo didn't exist, if that much was true, what guaranteed that I did? If I didn't actually exist, then who was here, bright and early, barely awake in the barber's chair?

I must have fallen into a deep sleep.

"Kokura's here!" a voice said into my ear, startling me awake. It was Kayo. I looked over, and seated two chairs down, attended by a pair of reverent assistants, was Aijiro Kokura. The original lady killer. The cornerstone of our studio. A star among stars.

I couldn't help myself and jumped out of the chair to greet him.

"Good morning, Sensei!"

"Morning. Sleepy huh? It's tough being young."

Kokura winked at me, with a rakish glimmer in his eye.

Even through the mirror I was too bashful to look at him directly. No one knew his actual age, but judging from the fact that he was famous in the silent era, he had to be over fifty. His face was breathtaking. Handsome in a way that blended manliness and suppleness, the rugged and the placid, stoicism and feeling. He was the dream lover of generations of women, from fifteen to seventy, sneaking into their bedrooms every night like a sandman of love.

But in the pronounced daylight of the barber's mirror, Aijiro Kokura's excesses were evident. He was a living god, male beauty sublime, incapable of doing wrong, but he had committed one great sin: the sin of growing old.

He wasn't wearing any makeup; and while he had retained his silhouette, his skin had lost its tautness. Decay was evident. Thanks to expert makeup, subtle camera angles, and tricks with lighting, the creases under his eyes had been hidden from the public, but there was no hiding the wrinkles from this angle. Something in his big, beautiful eyes had begun to turn, like dark ripples approaching from the distance. His mouth had slackened, and unless he kept it firmly shut the youthful line of his bottom lip was lost.

His handsome face had become a dingy plaque, a place to hang a mask—the mask of the handsome face that he had lost.

I was struck by an unfathomable terror and looked back into the mirror.

The old barber shifted his attention to Kokura and stepped away from my chair. The only thing remaining in the mirror was my young face poking from the bleach-white sheet.

Kayo entered the frame. The real Kayo, who existed. With her hair in a bun and no trace of makeup, she brought her lips to my ear and smiled at me through the mirror. Her silver teeth flashed between her lips.

She whispered to me in a voice almost too low to hear but hot with zeal.

"Even when you're sixty, I'm still going to call you my handsome prince."